The Merchant of Venice

Sweet Cherry
Publishing

Published by Sweet Cherry Publishing Limited
Unit E, Vulcan Business Complex,
Vulcan Road,
Leicester, LE5 3EB,
United Kingdom

First published in the USA in 2013
ISBN: 978-1-78226-077-6

©Macaw Books

Title: The Merchant of Venice
North American Edition

Text & Illustration by Macaw Books 2013

www.sweetcherrypublishing.com

Printed and bound by Wai Man Book Binding (China) Ltd. Kowloon, H.K.

About
Shakespeare

William Shakespeare, regarded as the greatest writer in the English language, was born in Stratford-upon-Avon in Warwickshire, England (around April 23, 1564 1564). He was the third of eight children born to John and Mary Shakespeare.

Shakespeare was a poet, playwright, and dramatist. He is often known as England's national poet and the "Bard of Avon." Thirty-eight plays, 154 sonnets, two long narrative poems, and several other poems are attributed to him. Shakespeare's plays have been translated into every major existent language and are performed more often than those of any other playwright.

Shylock: He is a Jewish moneylender. He is shrewd and cunning, and disliked by everyone. He devises a clever plan to take his revenge on Antonio by demanding a pound of Antonio's flesh if he is unable to pay back the borrowed money on time.

Antonio: He is a trader and also a moneylender. He signs a contract with Shylock because of his love for his friend Bassanio. He is liked by everyone, unlike Shylock.

Bassanio: He is a gentleman and a friend of Antonio. He borrows money from Shylock through Antonio. Though Bassanio later comes to his friend Antonio's rescue, he proves not to be much help.

Portia: She is a wealthy lady and the wife of Bassanio. Disguised as a young male lawyer, she tricks Shylock into forgiving Antonio even when he has no intention of doing so. She is beautiful, witty, and intelligent.

The Merchant of Venice

Once upon a time in Venice, there lived a Jew called Shylock. Shylock was a moneylender. When people needed money, they would go to Shylock, and he would give

them whatever amount they asked for—but in return, he would not only fix a date and time when his money had to be paid back but also charge them very high interest.

This led to most people in the city disliking Shylock. His biggest enemy, however, was a man called Antonio, a noble

trader. Antonio, like Shylock, would loan people money whenever they asked him for it, but in return, he did not chase them to repay him, nor did he charge his borrowers any interest. Thus, whenever Antonio encountered Shylock on the streets of Venice, he would leave no stone unturned

in insulting him. Shylock,
being an evil, calculating man,
never said anything to Antonio
in return, but he was waiting
for the perfect opportunity to
humiliate and disgrace him.

Antonio was the kindest
man ever known in Venice.
Of his many friends, one was
extremely close to him. As a

matter of fact, they were so close that they were more like brothers. But this nobleman, Bassanio, had one vice—he could never live off his income. His expenses were always wider than his pocket, and sooner or later he would always have to come to Antonio for money— not that Antonio minded.

One fine day, Bassanio arrived at Antonio's house and told him that he had found a way of restoring his fortune. He had fallen in love with a noble heiress called Portia. Bassanio knew Portia's father, and every time he had gone to their house, he had

seen her. Over time, they had fallen in love. But Portia's father had died recently, and Portia had inherited his fortune. Bassanio had decided that he was going to propose to her and ask for her hand in marriage. However, there was a problem. He wanted

to wear some fashionable new clothes for the occasion and, as usual, did not have any money. So he had come to borrow the sum of three thousand ducats from Antonio.

Antonio was overjoyed on
hearing what Bassanio had to
say. But at that moment he did
not have much money with
him. Some of his ships were to
return from their voyages in
a few days' time and then he
would have enough money to

lend to his friend, but he knew
the matter could not wait until
then. So he decided to go to
Shylock and borrow the money
from him to give to Bassanio.

Bassanio was not happy with
the idea, but Antonio insisted
that there would be no problem,

as his ships were due to return
soon. Once they reached Shylock
and told him they needed to
borrow some money, Shylock
realized that it was the moment
he had always been waiting for.
He told Antonio that though
he had always insulted him
in public, Shylock had always

wanted them to be friends.
Antonio was a little taken aback.
Shylock went on to tell him
that to show his good intent, he
would not only lend Antonio
the three thousand ducats but
also not charge him any interest.
All Antonio would have to do
in return was go with him to a

lawyer and sign a bond, which
would state that in the event

Antonio was unable to pay him back the money within a certain amount of time, Shylock would take a pound of flesh from any part of Antonio's body he desired.

Bassanio was not very happy with this proposal and begged Antonio not to put himself in any danger because of him. But Antonio felt that

he had misjudged the Jew all along and that his intentions were genuine, so he immediately agreed to sign the bond.

Finally, Shylock made the required payment to Antonio. With this money, Bassanio obtained some fashionable

clothes for himself and, with
another gentleman friend called
Gratiano, left for Portia's house.

Within a few moments,
Bassanio was able to get Portia to
agree to his proposal. He told her
that all he had was a noble name
and birth, but not much money.

Portia told him in return that
to be worthy of him, she would
have to be a thousand times
wealthier than she already was.
Presenting a ring to Bassanio,
she mentioned that all her wealth
and her property, along with her
own self, now belonged to him.

Meanwhile, Gratiano had
fallen in love with one of Portia's

companions, Nerissa. As Portia
and Bassanio were exchanging
vows of love, Gratiano walked up
to them and congratulated the
happy couple. He then
informed them that
he too would like to get
married. He explained
that Nerissa would
love to marry him,
but only when Portia
had married Bassanio.
So Bassanio and
Portia congratulated
the happy couple,
Gratiano and Nerissa.

While the
two couples were
merrily talking

about their fortunate affairs,
a messenger arrived at Portia's
house with extremely sorrowful
news. All of Antonio's ships,

which were expected to arrive in a short while, had been lost at sea. The noble Antonio was now penniless.

Bassanio was completely shattered by this news. He told Portia how Antonio would always lend him money whenever he needed it, and also

about the deal between Antonio
and the Jew. Seeing Bassanio
turn pale at Antonio's message,

Portia told him to make haste to Venice and free Antonio from the bond immediately. She also insisted that Bassanio marry her, for then he would have a legal right over her money, which he could use to free Antonio.

So, a marriage was arranged with great haste, and Bassanio

and Gratiano were married to their beloved ladies. Shortly, both men set off for Venice. Upon arriving in the city, Bassanio was shocked to find that Antonio was in prison.

Although Bassanio immediately sought out Shylock to pay him the money and release Antonio, there was a legal problem in the whole affair. It turned out that even with all the gold in the world, Bassanio would not be able to help Antonio, for the legal bond

clearly stated that in the event
that Antonio was unable to pay
the amount, Shylock would take
a pound of flesh from any part
of Antonio's body he wanted.
So no one could save Antonio

and he would have to die. A day had been fixed to present the matter before the Duke of Venice, where it would be settled and the punishment given.

Meanwhile, Portia, who had sent her husband to Antonio's aid, knew that it was going to be very difficult for him to release his friend from prison. She realized that to save him, she would have to do something herself. Without wasting any more time, she made haste for Venice.

Portia's father had a very close friend who was a counselor in law. To this gentleman Portia wrote a letter explaining the matter. The lawyer sent his counselor's robe, which she would have to wear in court, along with a letter, which explained what she should do in order to save Antonio.

So finally, Portia arrived
at the court at the appointed
time, dressed as a man in the
counselor's robe. She had also
brought Nerissa with her, who
was also dressed as a
man and came as the
counselor's clerk.

They presented
themselves before the

duke and handed him a letter from Portia's counselor, stating that he could not make it that day because of an illness—instead, he had sent these young lawyers to fight the case on his behalf. And so the case began.

At first, Portia tried to reason with the evil Shylock. She begged him to show mercy and forget all about the bond. She tried to

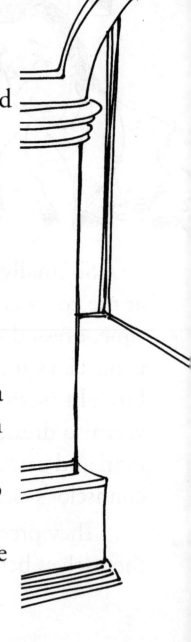

tempt him by saying that mercy
helps both the person granting
it and the person to whom
it is granted. But nothing
could change Shylock's mind.
He insisted that since it was
written in the bond, he should
be allowed to draw a pound
of flesh from Antonio's body.
That was all there was to it.

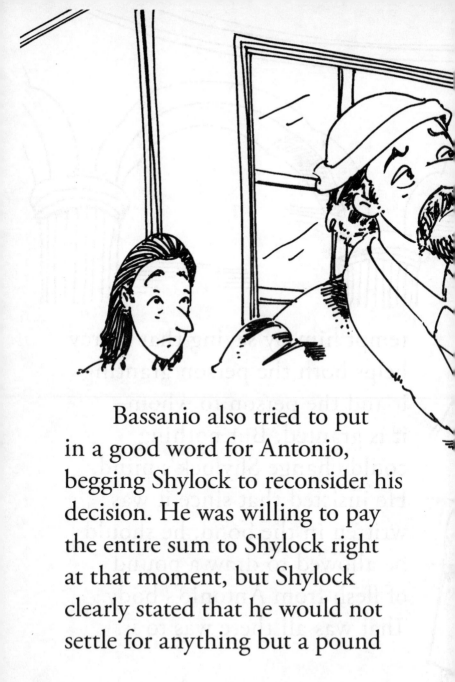

Bassanio also tried to put
in a good word for Antonio,
begging Shylock to reconsider his
decision. He was willing to pay
the entire sum to Shylock right
at that moment, but Shylock
clearly stated that he would not
settle for anything but a pound

of flesh, because it was stated
so in the legal agreement.

Portia then asked the court
if at least a surgeon could be
present when Shylock cut out a
pound of flesh from Antonio's
body. After all, Antonio could

bleed to death. But that was exactly what Shylock wanted. So he stated that since that clause was not in the bond, a surgeon could not be present when Shylock carried out his part of the deal.

Finally, Portia had no option but to agree to Shylock's proposal. She declared that the law indeed could not be bent and Shylock was entitled to demand his pound of flesh.

So she turned to Shylock and said, "Take

your pound of flesh, but without dropping a single drop of blood. And remember, you have to take a pound exactly, no less, no more."

Now Shylock was in a fix. How could he cut a piece of Antonio's body and yet there not be a drop of blood? And how on earth could he be so

accurate as to cut out exactly a pound of flesh? But Portia was now adamant that the bond stated that only a pound of flesh was to be taken and nothing more. And in the event that Shylock did not adhere to his part of the deal, she made it very clear that half of his property would go to Antonio and the

remaining half would be given
to the state of Venice as a penalty.

There was no escape for
Shylock now. He did not know
what to do. He tried to say that
he would be happy with his
money, but Portia reminded
him that the question of money
was irrelevant, as Shylock
himself had already stated.

Antonio said that he would be content if half of Shylock's wealth, which was to be handed over to him, went to Shylock's own daughter. Antonio knew that Shylock's daughter had married a

Christian and so Shylock had excluded her from his will.

Shylock, unable to speak another word, claimed that he was ill and begged to leave. He told the court that they should draw up a contract and have it sent to him. He would then

sign it at his house. So saying, the evil Jewish moneylender fled from the court, outsmarted by the young lawyer.

The duke freed Antonio from bondage and even praised the young lawyer whose efforts had set Antonio free. He asked Bassanio and Antonio to make the payment of three thousand ducats to the young man. While Bassanio readily agreed, Portia did not and declined the offer of money.

But when Bassanio took off
his glove and revealed the ring
that Portia had given him when
they got married, the young
lawyer promptly asked for it
back, wanting to have some
fun with Bassanio. Bassanio,
who obviously did not know
that the lawyer was none other
than his wife, was reluctant to
give the ring away.

But the lawyer would
not take anything else from
Bassanio except the ring. Antonio
then requested Bassanio give
the ring away, saying, "Let
him have the ring. Let my
love and the great service that
he has done for me be valued
against your wife's displeasure."

Bassanio obviously did not
want to dishonor his friend,
so he gave the ring away.

Nerissa also played the game
with Gratiano and took his ring
as well. Both the ladies laughed
as they left the courtroom, as
they could now have some fun
at their husbands' expense.

When they returned home, Portia and Nerissa changed into their usual attire and awaited the arrival of their husbands. Soon, Bassanio and Gratiano came back, along with Antonio. As Bassanio

was introducing Antonio to his wife, they heard a fight break out between Gratiano and Nerissa.

On being asked the reason for their argument, Nerissa told them that Gratiano had handed

over the ring to some clerk, a
ring he had refused to part with
when Nerissa gave it to him.
Gratiano tried to explain why
he had given the ring away and
told the ladies the whole story.

But Portia, who also wanted
to have some fun at Bassanio's

expense, reprimanded Gratiano
and told him that he was still
in the wrong for giving away
the ring. Her husband would
surely never do a thing like that,
she said. But Gratiano, in order
to shift the blame away from
him, told Portia that Bassanio

had first given his ring away,
and that was the only reason he
had given his own ring away.

Portia appeared to be
very angry upon hearing this.
Bassanio tried to pacify her
and told her the whole story

again, but she refused to listen
to his explanation. Antonio
lamented as to how he was the
reason behind this feud. Had it
not been for him, the married
couples would not be warring
like this. He then tried to calm
Portia down by telling her that

Bassanio would always be true to her, and he himself would be the guarantor of that.

So Portia handed Antonio a ring and told him to give it to his friend, and to tell him that he should not give this one away to anyone again. Bassanio was amazed to see the ring, because it was the very one that he had given to the young lawyer. Only then did he realize that the counselor

of law who had defended Antonio and saved his life was none other than his wife.

As the happy couples were rejoicing, a messenger came with the news that all of Antonio's ships that had been presumed lost had come into the harbor. Antonio was once again a rich man!